The Impact of God's Word on You

"It is the Spirit who gives life; the flesh profits nothing. The words that I speak to you are spirit and they are life." (John 6:63 NKJV)

By

Jennifer Nakuda

First printing 2021

Second printing 2025

USA Contact:

Tel: +1 945 304 3959

Email: jeniffern2000@gmail.com

Visit my social media:

Instagram: Jennifer Nakuda Author

Facebook: Jennifer Nakuda Author

Miracle Center Embassy

Arua, Uganda

Tel: +256 772612656, +256 703656873,

Email:, franknankunda@gmail.com

Copyright © 2021

Dedication

I humbly take this grand opportunity to appreciate the man of God who has had the greatest influence upon our lives and ministry through the years, Rev. Chris Oyakhilome, DSc., DD. Thank you, dear man of God for always teaching us the timeless truth of God's word in its simplest form, hearing you has brought out the best of God in us. I am forever grateful to God for you, Sir. I love you dearly, and pray for you always.

* * *

Acknowledgments

This book wouldn't be possible without the overwhelming inspiration of the Holy Spirit. What a privilege and an honor to have the word of God compiled for us in one book, to know and revere God in his majesty.

I'm grateful to every minister of the gospel, who has had a great impact in my life teaching and admonishing me in the word of God. Your investment in me is sure unto eternity. You were able to open my eyes to the reality of our kingdom and His Majesty the king, including us His royal subjects. For this, I am forever grateful. God bless you all for me!

A big thank you to Bookwave Publishing for a job well done in refining my words, designing the cover page and publishing a beautiful piece of work.

And of course, a mega thank you, to my dear husband, for the unwavering support always. Thank you very much.

* * *

About the Author

Jennifer Nakuda is an ordained Pastor and co-founder, alongside her husband, Frank Nakuda, of Miracle Embassy Church in Uganda, East Africa. Since 2003, she has served in various capacities within the church ministry. Inspired by her interactions with people from all walks of life, Pastor Jennifer has authored six books, offering practical guidance on living a purposeful and fulfilling Christian life. Outside of her ministry work, she is inspired by the beauty of the natural environment, enjoys traveling, and values quality time with family and friends.

Let us connect on Facebook, Instagram, or via email: jeniffern2000@gmail.com

* * *

Table of Contents

Introduction
What is prayer?

In his encounter with the devil, Jesus revealed a deep secret of all time, when the devil told him to turn stones into bread and Jesus said, *"Man shall not live by bread alone BUT by every word that proceeds from the mouth of God"* (Matt 4:4). In other words, he was saying that food is not the ultimate sustainer of man's life but the word of God.

The word of God created everything there is in existence (John 1:1-3) including man, and more especially, the born-again Christian in Christ. *"Being born again, not of corruptible seed, but of incorruptible, by the word of God, which liveth and abideth forever."* (1 Peter 1:23). The life we have in Christ is from the eternal living word of God; and because every living thing must stay connected to its source to stay alive, we too must stay plugged into the word of God to remain alive.

Jesus said, *"… the words I speak unto you, they are spirit, and they are life"* (John6:63) and then told the Jews that believed on him, *"If you abide in my word, you are my disciples indeed."* (John 8:31).

Moses, while talking to the children of Israel, cautioned them to set their hearts on the word that God gave them, saying it was their life and through it they would sustain their days wherever they went. He said, *"Set your hearts unto all the words which I testify among you this day, which ye shall command your children to observe to do, all the words of this law. For it is not a vain thing for you; because it is your life and through this thing ye shall prolong your days in the land, whither ye go over Jordan to possess it."* (Deut 32:46-47).

The word of God is not mere words; Moses said it is not a vain thing; it is your life and through it you shall prolong your days. Jesus said it is spirit, and it is life. It is what it says it is. God himself said, *"So, shall my word be that goes forth from my mouth; it shall not return to me void, but it shall accomplish what I please, and it shall prosper in the thing for which I sent it."* (Isaiah 55:11)

The most amazing truth about the word of God is the fact that it does not only give you knowledge; but as spirit and life, when you receive it, it mingles with your spirit at the same time renewing your mind to bring you into oneness with itself. Thereafter, it makes a lasting impact in and with your life. Just like we eat food and grow to become adults without ever knowing how the entire process takes place within us, so does the word of God impact our lives to produce in us character, beauty, excellence, faith, grace, wisdom, health, wealth and much more. Everyone else will only see the transformation and wonder how you came about the greatness and success.

Apostle Paul, while talking to his son in the Lord Timothy, cautioned him to give himself entirely to the word, mediating upon it continually so that his profiting may appear to all. (1 Tim 4:13-15). It is evident that there is visible proof of God's word working and impacting the lives of those, who committedly give themselves to the Word.

King David testified how God had made him a wonder to many (Psalms 71:7). But we all know how King David delighted in the word of God, and made the Word his refuge. He always acknowledged how the word of God was the light that guided his way, saying, *"Your word is a lamp to my feet and a light to my path."* (Psalm 119:105).

Being born again by the word, we have no other way to live a great, beautiful, successful, and excellent life than living in the word of God that gave birth to us in Christ. It is submission to stay connected to the word of God, as the only true light that guides us through life.

We are cautioned to see life through the word, as the only way to live the Christian life, because though we are in the world, we are not of the world. Jesus emphasized this on several occasions, so we should know and never live our lives according to the standards of this world that are limited.

The standards of this world program the people to live in uncertainty, not sure about their tomorrow. They are always frightened by everything they hear, see and feel because they are still living in the fallen nature of sin and death. That's why Jesus, while praying for the church, said, *"They are not of the world, just as I am not of the world. Sanctify them by your truth, your word is truth. As you sent me into the world. I also have sent them into the world."* (John 17:16-18). He made it clear we are not of the world, and his word, which is truth, sanctifies us of any influence from world. However, He sent us into the world to tell them the good news of Christ's saving grace, so they can come out of the darkness into the light.

The word of God is our life. Everyone that desires to live the life of God in fullness, gets to the Bible. He said, *"If a man loves me, he will keep my words: and my Father will love him, and we will come unto him and make our abode with him."* The way God makes his abode in the lives of those who love him is by his word. God and His word are one (John 1:1).

If the word of God will dwell in you richly, life will cease to be a mystery. Joy and peace become your way of life. Always knowing you can do all things through Him, who strengthens you. You lead a life guided by wisdom, having no care in the world knowing, "greater is He that is in you than he that is in the world."

God told Joshua at the beginning of a seemingly very difficult assignment handed over to him from Moses, saying, *"Only be strong and very courageous, that you may observe to do according to all the Law, which Moses my servant commanded you; do not turn from it to the right hand or to the left, that you may prosper wherever you go."* (Joshua 1:7). It doesn't matter where we find ourselves in this great world, if we will not turn from the book to the left or right, but courageously do what it says, success and greatness is guaranteed.

It is my prayer therefore, that as you read this book, you will be inspired by what I consider to be the four major blessings of the word of God in our lives. I pray, it will not be just a read but a stirring up of your righteous soul to fall in love with His word.

* * *

Chapter 1
The Word of God Shows You, Who You Are in Christ and Transforms You into the Image that You See

One of the most exciting discoveries in the word of God is seeing ourselves in the scriptures and finding out that God knew us before we ever came and planned a great life for us. The Bible says in Romans 8:29 AMP, **"For those whom He did foreknew (of whom He was aware and loved beforehand), He also destined from the beginning (foreordaining them) to be molded into the image of His Son (and share inwardly His likeness), that He might become the firstborn among many brethren."** Did you see that? God knew us before we came on the scene and planed that we should be like his dear Son, conformed to his image; so that Jesus Christ would be the first born among us, his many brethren everywhere. Hallelujah!

This literary means that if you are a born-again Christian, the picture of Jesus you see in the scriptures, is God's vision of you. It's the very image God sees you to be.

* * *

As He Is, So Are We In This World

The Spirit of the Lord through Apostle John reveals to us a fundamental truth about our true identity in 1 John 4:17 saying, *"...as he is, so are we in this world."* Yes, as Jesus is now, so are we in this world. Not when we get to heaven, but now, in this present world. Not the Jesus who walked the streets of Galilee before death, but the glorified Jesus after resurrection. This is mind blowing. But if your spirit can grasp it, your mind will be renewed.

Jesus became a sinner like us in order to die in our place. The bible says we all (everybody in the world) died in him on the cross, and when he rose again from the dead, we (everybody in the world) rose again with him to a new life. (Romans 6:3-11). When you believe this, and accept him as your Lord and savior, this truth becomes a vital reality in your life. You receive this new life, called eternal life in your spirit. This is the very life of God that we share with him. The new life after Jesus' resurrection.

When Jesus walked this earth, he demonstrated a life beyond this world, that's the very life he came to give whosoever believes in Him. When he rose from the dead, it became possible to impart this life of God in the hearts of those who believe in Him. This life of God in our hearts, makes it possible for us to be like him in the earth; and so, the Bible says, "As He is so are we in this world." This then means when you see him in the scriptures, as He is today after resurrection, you are seeing you! Remarkable indeed!

The Bible shows a very big difference between the Jesus before death and the Jesus after resurrection. The Jesus after resurrection surpasses in glory, power and authority. The Bible says as He is now after resurrection, so are we in this world. The glory of the resurrected Jesus is the glory we received in Christ. ***"For whom He did foreknow, He also did predestinate to be conformed to the image of his son, that he might be the firstborn among many brethren. Moreover, whom he did predestinate, them he also called, and whom he called them he also justified, and whom he justified, them he also glorified."*** (Romans 8:29-30).

That's why the Bible says, "If any man be in Christ, he is a new creation. (2Cor 5:17). One that has never existed before. One that is as He is. One that is one spirit with Him. ***"But he who is joined to the Lord is one spirit with him."*** (1Cor 6:17). Think about this! You are one spirit with the Lord. And we are all together, the church, his body, himself being the head. (Eph 1:22-23).

Our likeness and oneness cannot be more emphasized than being His body, flesh and bones. *"For we are members of his body, of his flesh, and of his bones."* (Eph 5:30) Can you see that this is one person? He is the head we are his body. He is in us, and we are in Him. That's the church of Jesus Christ. That's why on encountering Saul going after the church, Jesus didn't ask him why he was persecuting his followers, instead, he straightly asked Saul, "Why do you persecute me?" (Acts 9; 4-8) Simply because "As he is, so are we in this world."

We were brought into fellowship with Jesus Christ (1Cor 1:9). It is a fellowship of communion, a mingling together that brings us into a oneness that causes us to see, think and talk like him because we have the mind of Christ. (1 Cor 2:16). He made us partakers of his divine nature, having escaped the corruption that is in the world by lust. (2Peter 1:4). We have the same nature and life of God in our spirit (Ephesians 4:24).

Discovering who we are in Christ is very important in our Christian journey. It empowers us to live our lives in glory as God designed it. God is not impressed when we live our lives as though Jesus didn't come to give us eternal life. God wants us to find out and make sure we live that divine life we have in Christ, a life without limits, full of possibilities. It is not enough to know you are a child of God. We must know what it means to be born of God.

We are the manifestation of God's glory in the earth. People ought to see us and see the glory of God in our lives. Jesus said, *"I am the vine, ye are the branches..."* (John 15:5), certainly the vine and its branches are one and the same, having the same life. The branches are the fruit bearing part of the vine and that's who we are; called to show forth the glory of our father in the earth by our fruits of righteousness.

The born-again Christian is the most beautiful, precious and glorified creature of God on earth today. It doesn't matter what the world thinks of us. The world cannot define us, because it doesn't know us in the same way it didn't know Jesus. But the most disturbing part is when the Christians don't know who they're in Christ and choose to live as ordinary men and women setting their affection on things in the world.

Yet the Bible has said, *"If ye then be risen with Christ, seek those things which are above, where Christ is seated on the right hand of God. Set your affection on things above, not on things on the earth. Ye are dead and your life is hid with Christ in God. When Christ who is our life appears, then you also will appear with Him in glory."* (Col 3:3). We died to the world and our lives are hid with Christ in God. We have no other life but the one in Christ. *"In him we live, and move, and have our being…"* (Acts17:28). We have been raised together with Christ and made to sit together in heavenly places in him (Ephesians 2:6).

Apostle Peter, by the Spirit of God, describes us, saying, *"Ye are a chosen generation a royal priesthood, a holy nation a peculiar people; that ye should show forth the praises of him who has called you out of darkness into his marvelous light."* (1 Peter 2:9). This is exactly what God wanted the children of Israel to become in the earth if they obeyed his voice. (Exodus 19:5-6). But to the new creature in Christ, he says you are now that peculiar people, a chosen generation, a kingdom of priests and a holy nation. All because we believed in Jesus Christ as Lord and savior. And as his holy nation now, we are called to manifest his excellencies and glory everywhere we are in this beautiful world. *"For we are his workmanship; created in Christ for good works, which God prepared beforehand that we should walk in them."* (Ephesians 2:10).

If you don't study the Bible after you are born again, you might be deceived to think you simply joined a religion or a group of people that believe in

Jesus and that is all. Jesus said, *"If you continue in my word, then are you my disciples indeed. And you shall know the truth, and the truth shall make you free."* (John 8:31-32) The reason for continuing in the word is for us to be free from ignorance and know who we have become in Christ, who we have believed and why we are here, so we can live the Christ life in fullness. Life becomes meaningful after discovering our true identity and choosing to live it.

* * *

Conforming to His Image

Discovering who we are in Christ, makes one truth clear, that as He is, so are we in this world. This then drives us to know who He is so we can live our lives accordingly. Just because a baby is one day or six months, and can't talk, walk or run, doesn't mean he is not a full human being. He is as much human as his parents are. What needs to be done is to feed him to grow and develop his human characteristics.

In the same way, when we come to Christ, we are fully as He is, sharing his life and nature but still babies who need to be feed to grow and develop our spirituality. *"As newborn babies, desire the sincere milk of the word, that ye may grow thereby: if so be ye have tasted that the Lord is gracious."* (1 Peter 2:2-3).

We have to understand that as born-again Christians we have been called to conform to the image of Christ. God's dream and greatest desire for his children is to see us all conformed to the image of his son. Only when we are conformed to his image can we live to our full potential as sons of God in this world.

That is the reason, *"He gave some apostles; and some prophets; and some evangelists; and some pastors; and teachers; for the perfecting of the saints, for the work of the ministry, for the edifying of the body of Christ; till we all come in the unity of the faith and of the knowledge of the Son of God, unto a perfect man, unto the measure of the stature of the fullness of Christ; that we henceforth be no more children tossed to and fro and carried about with every wind of doctrine, by the sleight of men and cunning craftiness whereby they lie in wait to deceive; but speaking the truth in love may grow up into him in all things which is the head even Christ."* (Ephesians 4:11-15).

God appoints ministers over us to nurture us through the word from babyhood to a full-grown man or woman in Christ. He decides if your minister is an apostle, a prophet, a teacher, a pastor, etc. We don't choose church for fleshly reasons. It is a spiritual connection that supernaturally connects us to that minister that God has appointed over us, and we find ourselves at home under his/ her ministry.

When we yield to that spiritual leadership and actively participate in the work of the ministry under that minister, totally observing the word of God; our spiritual progress can only be evident for all to see. Our life becomes extraordinary, and the scripture is fulfilled that says, *"And nothing shall be impossible unto you."* (Matt 17:20). Success, greatness and excellence become your life experience, and you talk like King David 'God has made me a wonder to many.' (Psalms 71:7).

The secret of the Word is simple. The more we give ourselves to it; to study and listen to it continually, the more we become like what it talks about. We don't have to try hard to walk in the word, we only open our hearts to the word, like paying attention while listening or studying, and it does the transformation by itself. Then you find your life is continually guided by the word of God in the right paths you should follow. The more we yield to the word to live by it, the more glory we enjoy in our lives and the image of Christ that is formed and seen in us. Just as the Bible says, *"And all of us, as with unveiled face, {because we} continued to behold {in the word of God} as in a mirror the glory of the lord, are constantly being transfigured into His very own image in ever increasing splendor and from one degree of glory to another, {for this comes} from the lord {who is} the Spirit."* (2 Corinthians 3:18 AMP).

We should know that conforming to the image of Christ doesn't just happen to a Christian as the years go by; it is a personal decision from a hungry heart desiring spiritual growth and conformity to the master. Apostle Peter says, *"Wherefore laying aside all malice and all guile, and hypocrisies, and envies, and all evil speaking, as new born babies, <u>desire the sincere milk of the Word that you may grow thereby.</u>"* (1 Peter 2:1-2).

The Book of Hebrews 5:12-13 talks about brethren that were expected to have been teachers at a particular time but were found in need of someone to teach them the foundations of Christianity again. They still needed the spiritual milk because they had not given themselves to the Word to grow. *"For when for the time ye ought to be teachers, ye have need that one teaches you again, which be the first principles of the oracles of God; and are become such as have need of milk, and not of strong meat. For every one that uses milk is unskillful in the word of righteousness for he is a babe."*

Paul experienced the same, when he visited the Corinthian church and could not speak to them as spiritual or mature Christians because they were still babies in Christ. *"And I brethren, could not speak unto you as unto spiritual, but as unto carnal, even as unto babes in Christ. I have fed you with milk, and not with meat: for hitherto ye were not able to bear it, neither yet now are ye able. For ye are yet carnal: for whereas there is among you envying, and strife, and divisions, are ye not carnal and walk as men? For while one says, I am of Paul; and another, I am of Apollos; are ye not carnal?"* (1Cor 3:1-4).

The most visible characteristic of babies is their inability to talk right, followed with doing things the wrong way. It was evident that these guys at the Corinthian church had not given themselves to the Word to grow. Their talk and works of strife, envy and divisions proved it. Paul described them as carnal walking like mere men ,because as children God they are not supposed to be like mere natural men.

For example, it is not uncommon to find Christians of many years making statements contrary to who they are in Christ. They have never committedly given themselves to the word of God to change their mindset. Evil speaking in the scripture above is not necessarily the use of abusive words, but use of words contrary to one's new image in Christ. Phrases such as "I am broke' 'I am scared' 'I am dead, 'I am stressed', 'I am weak', or 'I am finished' that people speak, are termed as evil according to the scriptures. Remember the twelves spies that reported exactly what they saw in the land and built-up fear in the children of Isreal? The Lord called it an evil report. (Num 13:32). Evil words bind up people and keep them in a vicious circle of problems without knowing. It is a bleach in the spirit.

James says you are deceiving yourself. James 1:21-24, "Therefore lay aside all filthiness and superfluity of naughtiness, and received with meekness the implanted word, which is able to save your souls. But be ye doers of the word, and not hearers only, deceiving your own selves..." You are lying to your spirit and creating confusion in your life. Your spirit is awaked to God and sees a different picture but here you are saying something contrary to who you are in Christ. This explains the stagnation of many of God's children. They find it difficult to make progress, it's one step forward and another step backward. Today, they are happy and rejoicing in the word, the next day, they are talking fear.

Drinking the sincere milk of God's word will renew the mind to start seeing life from God's point of view. Just because you don't have money in your pocket doesn't mean you are broke. You're an heir of God (Rom 8:17), the cattle on a thousand hills belong to your heavenly father (Psalms 50:10); he will kill any number of it for you. This is what David knew when he said, "The Lord is my shepherd, I shall not want. He makes me to lie down in green pastures…" that's abundance consciousness brother! David was always conscious of God's provision, not the emptiness of his pocket or bank account. Our fellowship with the word of God instills in us a godly mindset and vocabulary that agrees with the word of God keeping us in perpetual victory.

The changes that the children of God so desperately desire in their lives can be realized through the studying of scriptures. The so-called addictions, and fears, can all be broken by the power of God's word. Create a personal daily moment with the word of God and watch your life go from glory to glory. If we want God to help us, we cannot look for him anywhere else apart from his word. In his word, we will find all the answers to life's questions, because God is his word.

If a child of God remains a baby in spiritual things, he will often find himself in bondage to the circumstances of this world even though he is as Christ is and is called to a life of glory and an heir of God. The Bible says, ***"Even so, we, when we were children, were in bondage under the elements of the world."*** (Galatians 4:3). Fear, depression, sickness, anxiety, and the uncertainties of life may hit them any time and wreak havoc as if they are not children of God; and they will think it is what happens to everyone. Some still think it's normal for a child of God to get sick and if it's God's will to be healed if not they die.

But when you give yourself to the word, you will put away childish thinking and stop your body from being wrecked by sicknesses and start enjoying divine health (Rom 8:11). This is one of the reasons we speak in tongues of the Spirit until the power flows through our bodies to keep healthy. If the sickness is caused by demons, cast them out don't baby-sit demons. If the sickness is caused by environmental, nutritional or hygiene issues then do something about it.

You are the custodian of your body and God needs your body alive and healthy. You can't be of any use to you or any one even to God when you are sick. Find the elders of the church to pray with you. The Bible says the prayer of faith shall save the sick. (James 5:13-15). Keeping your body healthy is your responsibility. Don't let the devil tell you that God is testing you with sickness.

It is the same thing with sin. When you give yourself to the Word, you stop giving excuses for sin in your life and get rid of it completely. You say bye-bye to the lesser things of life and move on to maturity. You discover sin is for the carnal man, the one walking like a mere man, the unskilled in the word of righteousness (1 Cor 3:1-3, Heb 5:12). Just like Jesus said, *"Ye err, not knowing the scriptures, nor the power of God"* (Matt 22:29), everyone who knows the scriptures and the power of God, sins no more.

We are called to live a life through the word of God. A life that is independent of the circumstances of this world but demonstrating the beauty and glory of our heavenly kingdom in the world. Every time we study the scriptures we behold his glory, and the Spirit transforms us into that very image we see, and this goes on from one level of glory to another. The more we look the more like him we become. To grow in him is to walk in glory, power and authority in the earth, where all things are possible with you.

It is our privilege as children of the kingdom to study the word of God and be able to see the mysteries of the kingdom. Jesus said, *"Because it is given unto you to know the mysteries of the kingdom of heaven."* (Matthew 13:10-17). This means, we can look into the Word and see, understand, and be transformed into what we find, because the same spirit of the word has given birth to us in Christ and lives in us (1 John 2:27). No child of God with the Spirit of God should say the Bible is difficult. He says, *"The entrance of your words gives light, it gives understanding to the simple."* (Psalms 119:130). Only pay, attention while listening or studying the word of God and the rest will be testimony after testimony.

* * *

Chapter 2
The Word Builds Our Faith Strong

Faith is defined for us in Hebrews 11:1 as ***"The substance of things hoped for being the evidence of things not seen."*** In other words, though I don't see this thing with my optical eyes, yet in my spirit, it is so real that it has become a tangible substance and nothing in this world can convince me out of its reality. Just like the dear man of God Pr. Chris Oyakhilome says, "Our faith is the ability to see the scriptures in pictures." How true!

It is not enough to just hear and believe or agree with the Word. Believing is good and it introduces us to a whole new world of possibilities. But acting on what we have believed is what is called faith; it is what unlocks the supernatural to flow in our lives. I dare say that it is not faith until you are moved to action. So then, we must keep hearing and hearing by the word until our spirit, soul, and body are overwhelmed by the word moving us to action.

Faith can be seen in our actions and heard in our words, especially, when we are caught off guard. Your immediate response when you hear bad news reveals if there is faith or not. Faith is not supposed be a formula that we pick up to use when trouble strikes, faith is supposed to be and is our way of life in Christ. "The just shall live by faith," says the scriptures. (Heb 10:38). It is our everyday life.

Our faith journey begun when we heard the gospel, believed it, and confessed Christ as Lord of our lives. We were not there when Jesus died, rose again, and ascended to heaven. Yet we believed in our spirit when we heard the salvation story and acted on our believing by confessing Him as our Lord and Savior; and immediately our spirits were awaked to the fatherhood of God. The miracle of salvation happened, and the Holy Spirit assures us deep in our spirit that we are children of God, born anew in Christ. (Rom 8:16).

That is how our faith life begun and there is no turning back. Our life in Christ is hinged on this principle of faith from start to finish. We believe in the scriptures and live our lives according to what the scriptures say. Faith became our ability to see a different life through the scriptures and choose to live that life without fear or shame. *"I am not ashamed of the gospel, because it is the power of God for the salvation of everyone who believes: first for the Jew, then for the Gentiles. For in the gospel a righteousness from God is revealed, a righteousness that is by faith from first to last, just as it is written: "The righteous will live by faith."* (Rom 1"16-17 NIV).

When we dare to believe the word of God, it drives us to action. In the word of God is the power that moves the one who believes to act. Whosoever opens up to the gospel receives the ability to believe and act on what they have believed — thus, faith is imparted through the gospel. (Rom 12:3). For example there are many people that have lived around Christians, and they proudly tell everyone how they grew up in a Christian home and carry a Christian name. But they have never taken the action to confess Christ as lord of their lives. They have not opened their hearts to the gospel to believe it and act upon it.

They may claim to love Jesus and also enjoy being religious, but until they believe in His sacrifice and confess Jesus as Lord of their lives, they are not born again, and God doesn't know them as his children. *"For with the heart man believes unto righteousness and with the mouth confession is made unto salvation."* (Rom 10:10). But of course, many are blinded by the god of this world who doesn't want them to see this glorious gospel of Christ. That is why we must pray that their minds be opened to the gospel, to believe it in their hearts and confess Jesus as Lord and savior of their lives. (2 Cor 4:4).

What we do in response to the Word we hear is what matters and proves our faith in God. Our response is very important in activating the flow of God's power to work in our lives. All the people that Jesus healed and experienced God's power had one thing in common — faith. They responded to the words they received. From their hearts they reached out to God saying, 'Yes, Lord I believe,' and they acted on their believing. Whatever action they took was faith in action. Whether they touched the helm of his garment, cried out to the son of David, stood up when he told them to carry their beds and go home, or climbed the tree to watch him pass by; it was faith in operation.

* * *

Building Strong Faith

The Bible says, *"**Faith comes by hearing and hearing by the word of God.**"* (Romans 10:17). The more of God's word we open our hearts to, the more faith that is stirred up in us to do the impossible. First and foremost, faith speaks. When faith is building up in our spirits, we start to say what we have believed. *"**We having the same spirit of Faith, according as it is written, I believed and therefore have I spoken; we also believe and therefore we speak.**"* (2 Cor 4:13). When faith is built up, we hear it in our words of courage and triumph that flow out of us freely without prior planning.

Faith is a force, and once faith is set in motion it can't be stopped by anything, it will surely produce results. Faith is not speaking positive words trying to get something; faith is speaking forth what you have already received in your spirit. The reason for speaking it forth is to bring it to the physical world. The reason we didn't see what we hoped for is simply because it wasn't real in our spirit. It was not yet a substance in our spirit.

There was a man that brought his son to Jesus' disciples to be delivered of a demon that often times threw him in the fire or water. The disciples tried to cast out the demon, but they couldn't until Jesus returned and cast out the devil from the boy. Then the disciple came privately to ask Jesus why they couldn't cast the demon out. Jesus frankly told them, *"Because of your unbelief. For verily I say unto you, if ye have faith as a grain of mustard seed, ye shall say unto this mountain, remove hence to yonder place; and it shall remove, and nothing shall be impossible unto you. Howbeit this kind goes not out but by prayer and fasting."* (Matt 17: 15-21).

The disciples must have believed they could cast out the demon, but they didn't, and Jesus said it was lack of faith. In other words, it was not real in their spirit, not yet a substance in their spirit. They must have done it, because they had seen Jesus doing it on several occasions, and assumed they, too, could cast out the demons by simply saying what he normally said in the way he said it. That's why they were surprised that the demon didn't go after doing everything in the same way Jesus always did. In desperation, they turned to Jesus and asked him why the demon didn't go.

The question then is, how do we make real what we are hoping for? Increase the knowledge of the scriptures through study and listening to God's word. Increasing the knowledge of the scriptures is very important and recommendable for every child of God who desires to walk in constant victory. The more of God's word in us, the more faith that is built up in our spirit. We said earlier that faith is a force. When faith is built up, it will drive you to action. You don't just say or do things because you heard the pastor or other Christians say and do them. You simply say and do things because you are moved from within your spirit that sees a different picture from what everyone else sees.

This is when you will take action and insist until you see in the physical, what you have seen in the spirit. You will pray until you have the answer.

You will add fasting to your prayer until you have the miracle. You will not rest until you see what you want. You may look like a crazy person making declarations and refusing to take a no for an answer, but it is faith in action that won't let go of the picture of the spirit. It is called the fight of faith (1 Timothy 6:12), where you refuse to give up or give in to the opposition. You hold on to what you know is supposed to be according to God's word.

Faith is acting the first time, the second time, the third time, to the seventh time, until we are told there is a cloud for a downpour. That's how Elijah caused rain to come down after three and half years of no rain in Israel. (1 Kings 18:43-46). We build our faith strong by acting on the scriptures we have believed as truth. If we have believed that the word of God is truth, then we practice it daily in our activities. Before long it becomes the only way, we know to live.

For example, before you run to pick the pain killer for the pain in your body, first rebuke the pain (Mark 16: 17-18). Before you rush to make that call to a friend or family for help, pray to the Lord for direction (Psalms 46). The more we practice the word of God at every given opportunity and see it produce results in our lives, the more our faith is strengthened and built strong for bigger challenges of life.

It is very important to have our faith built up strong at all times, because most situations of life require the already built-up faith; call it "The Now Faith," just like young David before Goliath the giant of Gath. David didn't have time to go back home for prayer and fasting. He had to deal with Goliath immediately. The giant was running out of patience asking for a challenger from the army of Israel.

Most times, there's a need for immediate action to save the future of a family, company, city or nation. Will your faith be found strong enough to make a difference?! What if you are the only hope they have? Training ourselves daily to live by the word of God builds in us a steadfastness of the spirit that turns on the flow of God's power every time the power of God is required to make a change.

* * *

David's Strong Faith

Take young David's example when he heard about Goliath the giant, who was threatening the whole army of Israel. David simply asked, *"What shall be done to the man that killeth this philistine and taketh away the reproach from Israel? For who is this uncircumcised philistine that he should defy the armies of the living God?"* (1 Sam 17:26). David, as young as he was, didn't complain being sent to the battlefield to check on his brothers, neither did he run away for his dear life to his father crying 'Daddy, the war is hotter than fire, lets pray for my bothers to survive.' No! Young David was bigger than that despite his age. He could not understand why the whole army of Israel was threatened by this one man. David was not bothered by the size of the giant or his threats. David knew something that the entire army of Israel and their king overlooked.

How did David come about this strong fearless faith? Some will say because he was anointed with oil. Oh, yes, I agree! But what about the children of God today who are not only anointed but have the Holy Spirit himself living in them, and yet, allow small scares from the enemy to give them sleepless nights — worrying and wondering what to do? Where is all the power in them hiding? Simple! Here is the answer! That power is activated by knowledge of God's word.

When the child of God knows so little of God's word, that power of the Holy Spirit will not be effectively used. Even in prayer, where that power is commonly stirred up, it is not put to good use, because people say the wrong things in prayer due to ignorance of God's word. For example, instead of asking, they complain (John 14:13-14), instead of commanding things and situations to change to their favor (Mark 11:20-26), they beg God, as if he has withheld things from them. (2 Peter 1:3).

David believed the story told to him as a young lad of their covenant with Jehovah. Daily, he pondered on those thoughts as he saw many Israelites circumcised to fulfill the covenant. He continued to gather more information about the covenant and what it meant for them. If you read about David, you will discover he was a meticulous person that never left anything to chance. In the process of time, he found out that according to the covenant, one Israelite was to kill a thousand, and two would kill ten thousand. He carried this truth in him until a bear appeared one day to eat the sheep, and David was like, you small thing, don't you know according to the covenant, I am ordained to kill one thousand enemies? The anointing in him was activated and he killed it. Question! How much of God's word concerning you, have you believed to be able to activate the anointing of God's Spirit that is resident in you?

On another occasion, he did the same thing to the lion that had grabbed one of the sheep. And now, when he was sent to take food to his brothers in war, lo and behold, one who was not circumcised, a philistine of Gath, was insulting the God of Israel and his army. David was filled with holy anger and vowed to kill Goliath, the giant of Gath. I believe David said to himself, "Goliath is only one man, and I am ordained to kill one thousand." The covenant doesn't say unless he is a giant. Read the story for yourself in 1 Samuel 17.

David took five stones to fight the fully armored giant but guess what? Because the anointing was stirred up in him, his first stone went straight to the eye of the giant! That one spot that was not covered and the giant went head down to the ground! That's the power of faith in the Word that activates the anointing of God's Spirit in us. David took Goliath's sword to cut off Goliath's head that he showed around to everyone as proof that the giant was no more. Knowledge of God's word builds our faith strong enough to activate the power of God's Spirit for the required changes.

Just like he had killed the bear and the lion, David had the assurance that he could kill the giant according to the covenant. I dare say that David wouldn't have killed Goliath if he had first run away from the bear and the lion that had come to eat the sheep. But, because he stood up to the bear and lion and defeated them, he proved the covenant. Therefore, when Goliath showed up, David knew without a shadow of a doubt that Goliath was going to be just like them animals — dead! He actually called Goliath a dead dog before killing him. As far as David was concerned Goliath was already dead, even before throwing the first stone.

The Bible highlights inspiring generals of great faith in the book of Hebrews, chapter 11, which was written for our learning. Just picking out a portion, it says, **"For by it (faith) the elders obtained a good report... Who through faith subdued kingdoms, wrought righteousness, obtained promises, stopped the mouth of lions, quenched the violence of fire, escaped the edge of the sword, out of weakness were made strong, waxed valiant in fight, turned to flight the armies of the aliens. Women received their dead raised to life again; and others were tortured not accepting deliverance that they might obtain a better resurrection."** (Hebrews 11:2, 8, 32-35).

Right after the faith hall of fame, the Spirit cautions us in chapter 12, saying, *"Therefore, since we are surrounded by such a huge crowd of witnesses to the life of faith, let us strip off every weight that slows us down, especially, the sin that so easily hinders our progress and let us run with endurance the race that is set before us. We do this by keeping our eyes on Jesus, on whom our faith depends from start to finish. He was willing to die a shameful death on the cross because of the joy he knew would be his reward. Think about all he endured, when sinful people did such terrible things to him so that you don't become weary and give up."* (Hebrews 12:1-3 NLT).

The Bibles says, *"No weapon that is formed against thee shall prosper; and every tongue that shall rise against thee in judgment thou shall condemn. This is the heritage of the servants of the Lord and their righteousness is of me, saith the Lord."* (Isaiah 54:14-17).

"What shall we then say to these things? If God be for us, who can be against us? He that spared not his own Son but delivered him up for us all, how shall he not with him also freely give us all things? Who shall lay anything to the charge of God' elect? It is God that justifies... who shall separate us from the love of Christ? Shall tribulation, or distress or persecution or famine or nakedness or peril or sword? ...Nay, in all these things, you are more than a conqueror through him that loved us. For I am persuaded that neither death, nor life, nor angels, nor principalities, nor powers, nor things present nor things to come, nor height, nor depth, nor any other creature shall be able to separate us from the love of God, which is in Christ Jesus our Lord." (Romans 8: 31-39).

"For which cause we faint not; but though our outward man perish, yet the inward man is renewed day by day. For our light affliction, which is but for a moment, works for us a far more exceeding and eternal weight of glory; while we look not at the things which are seen, but at the things which are not seen; for the things which are seen are temporal but the things which are not seen are eternal." (2 Corinthians 4: 16-18).

As we continue to feed on God's word and practice it every day, it eventually becomes the only way we know to live consciously or unconsciously. Our mind becomes programed to a new world of possibilities that no matter what happens, we just know we are more than conquerors. It is called living in God's realm of endless possibilities, above the limits, never shaken by anything. (Acts 20:32).

It is a choice we make, to grow our faith strong every day. Strong faith doesn't come by being a Christian for many years or by simply attending every church meeting. It is a personal decision made by those who want to see more of God's glory in their lives. Those who yield to the leading of the Holy Spirit to be men and women of the word, those who pay close attention to hear the word because faith comes by hearing and hearing by the word.

There is a big difference between hearing and listening. You can listen without understanding but when hearing, you understand and act. Those who simply listen to the word are like those in the parable of the Sower, who Jesus said the word of the kingdom to them is like seeds that fell by the wayside, and because they didn't understand it, the enemy came and stole it away. (Mathew 13:19).

If you will daily have personal moments meditatively hearing the word of God, speaking and declaring it to yourself, your spirit will be continually strengthened with might and your mind conditioned to God's thoughts. Then your path will be aligned according to your words, and nothing in the world can stop your success. This is what God told Joshua. "If you do this, you will make your way prosperous and you will have good success." (Joshua 1:8).

Don't keep quiet. Voice what you have come to believe as truth, according to the scriptures. Voice it in prayer and whenever you can. "Christianity is a ministry of talking." Don't let things happen by themselves. Don't just take what life gives to you, you can determine what comes to you by your words. Circumstances of life don't change with time. You make things happen by your words. Otherwise, what you don't want is what will happen and only get worse with time. We have received power to make things happen the way they should. Don't allow wrong things into your life. Don't accommodate sickness, poverty, or failure. You can be what you dream to be. In Christ the limits are removed.

Just like we confessed the Lord Jesus Christ and became born again, so do we voice out every blessing that God has given to us in Christ Jesus. Don't make the wrong confession because of what you see around you, stick to who you are and what you have in Christ according to the scriptures.

Learn to daily declare, I am blessed, I am full of power by the Holy Ghost, I am the righteousness of God in Christ Jesus, therefore sin has no power over me, I am full of wisdom, I know all things. I am guided by wisdom, there are no errors in my life. The grace of God multiplies in my life daily. The journey of my life is from glory to glory by the Spirit of God that lives in me… Speak what you want to see for all things are yours. (1 Corinthians 3:21).

* * *

Chapter 3
The Word of God is the Spirit of Wisdom in Us

While growing up as a young Christian, I read the story of Solomon and how he functioned in wisdom more than any man that ever lived. I was left speechless for what wisdom had made him. I straight away started praying for wisdom in my life. Wisdom became my ever number one prayer point for years, until I found out in the scriptures that *"Christ is made unto us wisdom."* (1 Cor 1:30). I was overjoyed. In other words, Jesus the word of God that became flesh and dwelt amongst us (John 1:14) is wisdom personified; therefore, receiving Jesus as Lord and Savior is receiving the wisdom of God into my life. Little wonder that Jesus, while talking to the Jews, referred to himself as the one greater than Solomon. (Matt 12:42).

I also found out that receiving Jesus as Lord and Savior meant being born again by the same word of God, *"Being born again, not of corruptible seed but of incorruptible, by the word of God, which liveth and abideth forever."* (John 1:23). Henceforth, I didn't have to ask for wisdom again because wisdom gave birth to me in Christ. All I needed was to yield to the word of God and turn on the spirit of wisdom in me. What a joy it was to discover this! There is nothing we can't know or do when we learn how to take advantage of the wisdom of God in us.

* * *

How to Walk in Wisdom Continually through the Word

Apostle Paul once drew young Timothy's attention to that one thing that he required in order to walk in wisdom. He mentioned something very instructive for everyone desiring to walk in wisdom, *"That from a child thou hast known the holy scriptures, which are able to make you <u>wise</u>... all scripture is given by inspiration of God, and is profitable for doctrine for reproof for correction for instruction in righteousness, that the man of God may be perfect, thoroughly furnished unto all good works."* (2 Timothy 3: 15-17).

Those who don't understand this truth keep asking for wisdom instead of walking in wisdom. When you know that the word of God is the wisdom of God, you learn how to yield to the word, and always walk in wisdom. This was King Solomon's secret. He knew how to embrace God's word. That is exactly how he received wisdom and became the wisest man that ever lived until Jesus came.

We know that God gave Solomon wisdom through words (1 Kings 3:11-14). I mean, he literary spoke to him moreover in a dream while sleeping. God didn't give Solomon anything to eat. He just spoke words in a dream and when Solomon woke up; he knew it was more than just an ordinary dream. He believed the dream; and as an act of faith, went to Jerusalem, stood before the Ark of the Covenant, offered up burnt offerings, and made a feast to all his servants celebrating what God had told him in the dream. Soon enough it was evident for all to see that Solomon demonstrated extraordinary wisdom.

Now, the very word that was spoken over Solomon making him wise, gave birth to us in Christ (James 1:18). Think how much wisdom we should be demonstrating in our daily lives. That is why he said, *"Let your light so shine before men, that they will see your good works and glorify your father in Heaven."* (Matt 5:16). The difference is in our response to the word. See how Solomon celebrated the word spoken to him in the dream and the quick manifestation of it.

Our response to the Word is very important and determines how the word is going to work in our lives. When did we last give an offering for the Word that touched our hearts like Solomon did? We must cultivate a culture that celebrates the word of God. The celebration seals the word in our spirits causing us to walk in the power of it. We are not strangers to the word of God, the Word gave birth to us and every time we receive the Word into our spirits, it is a spiritual union that turns on the flow of wisdom in our lives.

Jesus once told a parable of a wise and a foolish builder in Matthew 7:24-27, letting us know the importance of heeding his saying, *"Therefore, whosoever heareth these sayings of mine, and doeth them, I will liken him unto a wise man, which built his house upon a rock. And the rain descended, and the floods came, and the winds blew, and beat upon that house; and it fell not for it was founded upon a rock. And everyone, that heareth these sayings of mine and doeth them not, shall be likened unto a foolish man which built his house upon the sand. And the rain descended and the floods came and the winds blew and beat upon that house and it fell and great was the fall of it."*

God has given us his word to build our lives for an exceptionally excellent life on earth. Every wise child of God embraces the Word and builds a great life guided by wisdom. But the foolish ignores the Word and suffers for it. Jesus made it clear that the storms and challenges of life come upon all people, but the one established in the word of God will always remain standing in victory. By the wisdom of God's word, the wise always know how to prevent the trouble or come out of trouble. *"For wisdom is a defense, and money is a defense, but the excellency of knowledge is that wisdom gives life to them that have it."* (Eccl 7:12).

He said, *"In the world ye shall have many tribulations; but be of good cheer, I have overcome the world."* (John 16:33). He didn't say you will never face any challenge in this world. As a matter of fact, all troubles in this world are targeted towards you, the child of God, because you have chosen to live for God and not the devil in this world (2 Tim 3:12). But, Jesus said be of good cheer, because he overcame the world and gave us the victory. Through his word, he shows us how to keep the world and its system under (1 John 5:4). It is foolishness to ignore the word. You are unknowingly surrendering your life to the world; to be governed by its system and its chief, the devil. No matter how genuine your excuse may sound, Jesus only gave two options to either be wise or foolish. That is to either go the 'Word way' or the 'world way'.

If the devil can succeed in drawing you away from the Word, then he has you right where he can torment you and frustrate your life. Don't give him even a moment in your thoughts. Philippians 4:8 says, *"Finally, brethren, whatsoever things are true, whatsoever things are honest, whatsoever things are just, whatsoever things are pure, whatsoever things are lovely, whatsoever thing are of good report; if there be any virtue, and if there be any praise, think on these things."*

Wisdom says, whatever we allow to enter inside, is what will come out whether good or bad. Our lives are so much governed by what flows from inside us. If your heart is built strong on the Word — which is the wisdom of God — no force in the universe can overthrow you! David told Solomon, *"I have taught you in the way of wisdom; I have led thee in right paths, if you live a life guided by wisdom you won't limp or stumble as you run."* (Proverbs 4:11-12 NLT).

The more we interact with the word of God, allowing it to enter our hearts and renew our minds, the more wisdom we demonstrate in our daily lives. I mean, we just know the right thing to say and do, and have the willingness to say it and do it. Unlike the one who doesn't always yield to the Word. He may know the right thing to say and do but lacks the willingness and power to say it or do it.

The Psalmist always delighted in the word and testified of great wisdom. *"Oh, how I love your law! I think about it all day long. Your commands make me wiser than my enemies, for your commands are my constant guide. Yes, I have more insight than my teachers, for I am always thinking of your decrees. I am even wiser than my elders, for I have kept your commandments. I have refused to walk on any path of evil, that I may remain obedient to your word."* (Psalm 119:97-101 NLT).

Often the children of God find themselves in desperate need of hearing from God. But this is where it all begins because wisdom is the voice of God. If you will allow the word to lead you, you will always hear when God is talking because he constantly talks to us in every situation. His voice gets clearer as we spend more time with his word. (John 10:1-5).

Now, when you consistently pray in the Spirit, by the word of God, making declarations of God's word, wisdom becomes a force that flows in you continually, opening up reservoirs of spiritual wisdom and revelations that no man can find anywhere else but in the Spirit. Wisdom begins to lead your life to always do the right thing the first time. Error becomes a thing of the past and you become a perfect man in your ways. Wisdom positions you rightly, always finding yourself in the right place at the right time; and just like Daniel was preferred above all presidents and princes because of the spirit of excellence (Daniel 6:3), you will be preferred above all your peers because of the spirit of wisdom at work in you.

* * *

The Wisdom of God Vs. the Wisdom of This World

There's a very big difference between the wisdom of God and the wisdom of this world. Many live by the wisdom of this world and are faced with limitations and defeat in life. But being born again, we are translated from the wisdom of this world to divine wisdom. Divine wisdom gives you a divine understanding of life situations and shows you how to deal with them.

Divine wisdom enables you to see, interpret and understand things beyond what seems obvious and normal to the human eye. Divine wisdom shows you something good out of a hopeless situation. Divine wisdom sees the cancer dead when everyone else is planning for a burial. The wisdom of God will cause you to see a promotion where there is a termination letter.

Paul said, *"And my speech and my preaching was not with enticing words of man's wisdom, but in demonstration of the Spirit and of power. That your faith should not stand in the wisdom of men, but in the power of God. Howbeit we speak wisdom among them that are perfect; yet not the wisdom of this world nor of the princes of this world that come to naught; but we speak the wisdom of God in a mystery even the hidden wisdom which God ordained before the world unto our glory."* (1 Corinthians 2:4-7).

God planned before we ever came that we would walk in his wisdom for our glory. The wisdom of this world is limited but the wisdom of God is without limits. God's wisdom is not obvious, and neither is it revealed to everybody. It is for those who yield themselves to God's word to know his ways. He has made it possible for us through his word to see his wisdom in every situation and speak it forth. As we speak the wisdom of God, the situations change to align with God's perfect will and purpose in our lives, families, cities, etc. That's how we can live above the circumstances of life; by speaking the wisdom of God into life situations and cause them to align with God's perfect plan and will.

The devil's plan is to get you frustrated and discouraged by the situations of life, making you feel helpless. His desire is for you to turn to the wisdom of this world that offers seemingly easier options for a quick fix, but the end thereof is death. *"There is a way that seems right unto a man, but the end thereof are the ways of death."* (Pro 16:25). Jesus once asked, *"What shall it profit a man, if he shall gain the whole world and lose his own soul?"* (Mark 8:36).

As the scriptures say, *"I will destroy human wisdom and discard their most brilliant ideas."* So, where does this leave the philosophers, the scholars, and the world's brilliant debaters? God has made them all look foolish and has shown their wisdom to be useless nonsense.

Since God in his wisdom saw to it that the world would never find him through human wisdom, he has used our foolish preaching to save all who believe. God's way seems foolish to the Jews, because they want a sign from Heaven to prove that it is true. And it is foolish to the Greeks because they believe only what agrees with their own wisdom.

So, when we preach that Christ was crucified, the Jews are offended, and the Gentiles say that it's all nonsense. But to those called by God to Salvation, both Jews and Gentiles, Christ is the mighty power of God and the wonderful wisdom of God. (1 Cor 1:19-24 NLT).

Proverbs 8:1-21 have a beautiful excerpt of wisdom calling out to the children of men to heed her voice saying, *"I call to you, to all of you I am raising my voice to all people. How naïve you are! Let me give you common sense. O foolish ones, let me give you understanding.*

Listen to me! For I have excellent things to tell you. Everything I say is right, for I speak the truth and hate every kind of deception. My advice is wholesome and good. There is nothing crooked or twisted in it. My words are plain to anyone with understanding, clear to those who want to learn.

Choose my instruction rather than silver and knowledge over pure gold. For wisdom is far more valuable than rubies. Nothing you desire can be compared with it. I wisdom, live together with good judgment. I know where to discover knowledge and discernment.

All who fear the lord will hate evil. That is why I hate pride, arrogance, corruption, and perverted speech. Good advice and success belong to me. Insight and strength are mine. Because of me, kings reign, and rulers make just laws. Rulers lead with my help, and nobles make righteous judgments.

I love all who love me. Those who search for me will surely find me. Unending riches, honor, wealth and justice are mine to distribute. My gifts are better than the purest gold, my wages are better than sterling silver. I walk in righteousness, in paths of justice. Those who love me inherit wealth, for I fill their treasuries."

The Spirit says, *"Wisdom is the principle thing; therefore, get wisdom and in all thy getting get understanding. Exalt her and she will promote thee: she shall bring thee to honor when thou does embrace her. She shall give to thine head an ornament of grace; a crown of glory shall she deliver to thee."* (Proverbs 4: 7-9). It is not a difficult thing to find and walk in wisdom. All the wisdom of God is abundantly made available to us in his word that gave birth to us in Christ. We simply plug into the word of God and have a continuous flow of wisdom in our lives. Every one that desires to walk in wisdom gets to the word of God to be instructed and programed for a great life of wisdom and excellence. He says, *"Hear instruction, and be wise, and refuse it not. Blessed is the man who listens to me, watching daily at my gates, waiting at the posts of my doors. For whoever finds me finds life and obtains favor from the Lord: but he who sins against me wrongs his own soul; all those who hate me love death."* (Proverbs 8:33-36).

* * *

Chapter 4
The Word of God Delivers to You, Your Inheritance in Christ

In his farewell massage to the Ephesian brethren, Apostle Paul by the Spirit reveals a powerful secret to the church, letting us know how we can enjoy our rich inheritance in Christ. He said, *"And now brethren, I commend you to God and <u>to the word of his grace, which is able to build you up and to give you an inheritance</u> among all them which are sanctified."* (Acts 20:32). In other words, when we give ourselves to God, we should submit ourselves to his word, which is able to build us up and deliver to us our inheritance in Christ.

It is very exciting to know that we did not only receive forgiveness of sins but also an inheritance in Christ. The Lord made Paul's mission to the gentiles very clear; *"To open their eyes and to turn them from darkness to light and from the power of Satan unto God that they may receive forgiveness of sins, and inheritance among them which are sanctified by faith that is in me."* (Acts 26: 18). Paul often times shared about our inheritance in Christ, letting the church know that we are heirs of God; therefore, we should have nothing to glory in because all things are ours. *"Therefore, let no man glory in men. For all things are yours. Whether Paul or Apollos, or Cephas, or the world... all are yours and ye are Christ's and Christ is God's."* (1 Corinthians 3:21-23).

In Christ we inherited everything. Everything that Christ has is also ours. *"The Spirit himself bears witness with our spirit that we are children of God; and if children then heirs; heirs of God and joint heirs with Christ..."*

(Rom 8: 16-17). Joint heirs mean, we own everything equally with Christ. Jesus has 100% ownership, and we also have 100% ownership of everything that belongs to God.

This can only be so because, *"He who unites himself with the Lord is one with him in spirit."* (1 Cor 6:17NIV), and the Bible says, *"We are members of his body, of his flesh, and of his bones."* (Ephesians 5:30). He is the head, and we are his body that completes him (Ephesians 1:22-23). We are seated together in heavenly places in him (Ephesians 2:6). Everything he owns that the Father has given to him (John 3:35), we own it together in him. It cannot get any better than this apart from *"Giving thanks unto the father who has qualified us to be partakers of the inheritance of the saints in light."* (Col 1:12).

* * *

Our Inheritance in Christ

Our inheritance in Christ is enormous, unfathomable and everlasting. We have a very rich spiritual inheritance and since the spiritual rules the physical, everything else is at our command. Everything you can imagine and that which you may not imagine is ours in Christ (1 Cor 3:21)! The Bible says that God has blessed us with all the spiritual blessings, *"Blessed be the God and Father of our Lord Jesus Christ, who has blessed us with all spiritual blessings in heavenly places in Christ."* (Ephesians 1:3).

We inherited all the spiritual blessings in heavenly places in Christ. All of them are ours to enjoy and take advantage of. What an inheritance! The Bible says in Ephesians 2: 6 NLT, *"For he raised us from the dead along with Christ and we are seated with him in the heavenly realms – all because we are one with Christ."* Did you see that? We are currently seated together in him in heavenly realms. This means we have been raised to a position of power, authority and dominion beyond this world. That position in the heavenly realms the Bible says is *"Far above all principality, and power, and might, and dominion, and every name that is named not only in this world, but also in that which is to come."* (Ephesians 1:21).

Don't take your spiritual heritage lightly. It is everything you are as a child of God in Christ. This inheritance is all that you ever required to live a successful, glorious and impactful life on earth. We have been given all the authority and power of God by his Holy Spirit that lives in us (1 Cor 6:19), we can do all things. We have also received the most wonderful and powerful name of Jesus to live by (Col 3:17, Phil 2:5-11); and his precious word as our guiding light (Psalms 119:105). What more shall we say? He has also made us kings and priests unto God to reign in life; *"And has made us unto our God kings and priests and we shall reign on the earth."* (Rev 5:10).

* * *

Heirs of the World

The Bible says, *"For ye are all the children of God by faith in Christ Jesus, for as many of you as have been baptized into Christ, have put on Christ. There is neither Jew nor Greek, there is neither bond nor free, there is neither male nor female; for ye are all one in Christ Jesus. And if ye be Christ's, then are ye Abraham's seed and heirs according to the promise."* (Galatians 3:26-29). This means that if you are in Christ, you are Abraham's seed, and therefore, an heir according to the promise God made to Abraham.

"For the promise that he (Abraham) should be the heir of the world was not to Abraham or to his seed, through the law, but through the righteousness of faith. Therefore, it is of faith that it might be by grace; to the end the promise might be sure to all the seed not to that only which is of the law, but to that also which is of the faith of Abraham who is the father of us all." (Romans 4:13-16). That seed through the righteousness of faith is Jesus

Christ, and whosoever is in Christ has inherited the world according to the promise God made to Abraham.

We have to understand that in the beginning God gave the world to Adam to govern it. But Adam failed and the devil took the right over the world becoming the god or prince of this world system (2 Cor 4:4). However, God had a redemption plan through Abraham and his seed Jesus Christ. When Jesus finally came, and was about to die on the cross said, *"Now will the prince of this world be cast out."* (John 12:31-32), because Jesus was going to pay for Adam's sin.

And when the price was finally paid, the Bible says, *"And being found in fashion as a man, he humbled himself, and became obedient unto death, even the death of the cross. Wherefore, God also has highly exalted him and given him a name which is above every name; that at the name of Jesus every knee should bow, of things in heaven and things in the earth and things under the earth; and that every tongue should confess that Jesus Christ is Lord, to the glory of God the father."* (Philippians 2:8-11).

At the resurrection after defeating the devil (Col 2:15), Jesus became the new boss having obtained a name that is above every name in heaven, on earth and under the earth becoming the heir of all things (John 3:35). Therefore, if we are children of God; then are we heirs, heirs of God and joint heirs with Christ. (Rom 8:17). Because we are in Him, we are reigning in this world through Him (Rom 5:17).

It doesn't matter what the devil tries to do through his children in this world. His system of governance may still be in operation until his tenure is over; nevertheless, his system has no power over the children of God. (1 John 5:4). We live in a different realm in this world. Jesus said we are not of this world system and according to God, Jesus owns the world today, and the church of Jesus Christ has received all the power and authority to reign in Jesus' behalf, paralyzing, rendering powerless, and dominating the works of wickedness around us in our cities, nations and the world.

I will never forget a testimony of one dear sister living in a particular town not far from our capital city, where robbery had become the order of the day. Thieves had taken over the area, breaking into people's homes every night. The sister went into prayer with her family, and they cast out that wickedness to this day that robbery has never returned to that town.

As long as the church is still here on the earth, the devil has no power to do what he wants unless the church lets him. If the church stands in its position of authority and takes charge of things the devil can't do nothing. *"Behold I give unto you power to tread on serpents and scorpions and over all the power of the enemy and nothing shall by any means hurt you."* (Luke 10:19).

Let no one deceive you, this world and the seeming glory therein is nothing compared to the glory that we have in Christ and the excellent glory that shall be revealed at his appearing. The church of Jesus Christ; is the most glorious thing in this present world and has received all the power and authority to reign in this world. There is nothing in this world that you can't have.

Satan once tempted Jesus with the passing glory of the kingdoms in the world (Matt 4:8-10), and he still does that today with many of God's children (1John2:15-17), but you don't have to be tempted with what belongs to you already. You only need to know how to start enjoying your inheritance, because it is all in your power as the heir of God. You can be what you want in this world, go where you want, do what you want as a joint heir with Christ Jesus.

* * *

How to Enjoy Your Earthly Inheritance

Now, as an heir of God and a joint heir with Christ, your name is literary on everything in this world. This renders every lack and poverty mindset powerless. This truth empowers us to do what we ought to do to enjoy our inheritance knowing that all things are ours. What then must we do to enjoy our inheritance? The Spirit through Paul let out the truth for very child of God to heed. ***"And now brethren, I commend you to God and <u>to the word of his grace which is able to build you up and to give you an inheritance</u> among all them which are sanctified."*** (Acts 20:32). In order for the word of God to deliver to you the inheritance, it will first and foremost renew your mind to give you a blessed and abundance mindset where you see yourself blessed and living in abundance as an heir of God. Then your talk will become one of a blessed person seeing abundance everywhere. This will set in motion the right conditions for your inheritance to gravitate towards you.

Until you see yourself blessed and talk that way, you will not permanently enjoy your inheritance. Your life will keep going up and down wondering why you are not permanently living in abundance. Meanwhile, it is because you're still talking like a child, unskilled in the teaching of righteousness. When the money is running low in the bank, you say, "I am broke, I don't know how I will take care of my next bills." You still think your job, husband, father or mother is your source of provision. You are still a child in need of training for spiritual matters.

The Bible says in Galatians 4:1, ***"Now, I say that the heir as long as he is a child differs nothing from a servant, though he be lord of all; but is under tutors and governors until the time appointed of the father."*** The heir, though he owns it all, he's not different from a servant, because he is still a child talking confusion, he can't manage the estate. Therefore, he is given to tutors and governors to teach him how to manage his inheritance. That's why, ***"He gave some apostles and some prophets and some evangelists and*** *some pastors and teachers for the perfecting of the saints for the work of the ministry for the edifying of the body of Christ; till we all come in the unity of the faith and of the knowledge of the Son of God, unto a perfect man, unto the measure of the stature of the fullness of Christ. That we henceforth be no more children, tossed to and fro, and carried about with every wind of doctrine...*" (Eph 4:11-14).

God gave us ministers to nurture us through his word, raising us to spiritual maturity, able to enjoy all our inheritance in Christ. The word of his grace, like Apostle Paul puts it, renews our mind, eliminating the poverty and lack mindset; positions us correctly to see life through God's word and builds us strong to exercise our spiritual authority and take charge of things as the rightful heirs.

Joshua too was instructed to give himself to the word of God in order to lead the children of Israel into their inheritance. God told him, *"This book of the law shall not depart out of <u>thy mouth</u>, but thou shall <u>meditate therein day and night</u> that thou may <u>observe to do</u> according to all that is written therein for then thou shall <u>make thy way prosperous</u> and then thou shall <u>have good success</u>.*" (Joshua 1:8).

The Bible says, *"Blessed is the man that walks not in the counsel of the ungodly nor stands in the way of sinners nor sits in the seat of the scornful. But his delight is in the law of the Lord and in his law does he meditate day and night. And he shall be like a tree planted by the rivers of water that brings forth his fruit in his season his leaf also shall not wither and <u>whatsoever he does shall prosper</u>*" (Psalms 1:1-3). Did you see that? Whatsoever he does shall prosper. It does not matter what you decide to do, if you are one that delights in the word, you will prosper. Just imagine. It is not dependent on which business is booming in the city or your country. No, he says whatsoever you choose to do shall prosper.

It is true we have inherited all things, but it is those that delight in the word of God, meditating therein, to renew their minds and come into a closer walk with the Holy Spirit that enjoy the full inheritance from glory to glory. The Holy Spirit is the author of the word and the chief administrator of the inheritance. If you listen to him, he will guide and lead you into your own inheritance. He knows everything and can do anything.

* * *

Financial and Material Inheritance

No one walks with Him and lives in lack. King David said something so profound about God and His children's welfare in (Psalms 37:25), *"I have been young, and now am old; yet have I not seen the righteous forsaken, nor his seed begging for bread."* There is a difference between walking with God and knowing about God. Those who walk with God know his ways because walking with God means walking in His ways. The Bible says, *"He made known His ways to Moses, His acts to the children of Isreal."* (Psalms 103:7). Because he spent time with God, Moses got to know God's ways and he walked in them; thus, walking with God. But the children of Isreal simply saw the acts of God but had no knowledge of His ways. They complained and grumbled about everything, always angry with God for not doing one thing or another. They definitely didn't know His ways. Those who know his ways, don't complain or grumble, they simply do what Gods says should be done and have their lives aligned perfectly.

In Genesis 8:22 God made a decree after the floods saying, *"While the earth remains, seedtime and harvest, cold and heat, winter and summer. And day and night shall not cease."* Do you want to know how he came about this decree? It was when Noah from the floods stepped out of the ark onto the dry ground and with thanksgiving gave God an offering. The Bible says God Smelled a sweet savor from Noah's offering and his heart was moved to bless the Earth and made a decree that stands to this day. *"And Noah built an altar unto the Lord; and took of every clean beast, and of every clean fowl, and offered burnt offerings on the altar. And the Lord smelled a sweet savor; and the lord said in his heart, I will not again curse the ground any more for man's sake; for the imagination of man's heart is evil from his youth; neither will I again smite any more everything living as I have done. While the earth remains seedtime and harvest, and cold and heat, and summer and winter and day and night shall not cease."* (Gen 8:20-22).

Since then, seedtime and harvest became a fundamental spiritual principle in the earth just as day and night is. God said as long as the earth remains it shall not cease. Whatever you sow, you shall reap. Even God to get man back to himself, He gave His son. Jesus on several occasion taught about this principle to help man understand how man's world works. *"Give and it shall be given unto you; good measure, pressed down, and shaken together, and running over; shall men give into your bosom, for with the same measure that you use, it will be measured back to you."* (Luke 6:38).

Everything in the earth has the ability to multiply. If you want anything to multiply, sow it and it will come back to you in abundance. To stop anything from multiplying, just don't sow it. That's why everything God gives is a seed. It is you to decide if you will sow it for abundance. *"This most generous God who gives seed to the farmer that becomes bread for your meals is more than extravagant with you. He gives you something you can then give away, which grows..."* (2 Cor 9:10 MSG). God gives you seed and when that seed is sown, He causes it to multiply so you will have food for your benefit and more seeds to sow for abundance. The process goes on until you live in abundance and never know lack. If you are a Sower, you will multiply your blessings and increase your greatness in the earth. But if you're one who ignores sowing, you will soon run dry because you are running your life against a spiritual principle in the earth.

It appears like unless we release something, we can't receive anything. That's why those that have not released themselves to God can't receive the free gift of Salvation. He does not force salvation onto anyone in as much as he wants everyone to be born again. This is why we pray for men's hearts to be softened towards the gospel so they can give themselves freely to God.

Giving or sowing is therefore that spiritual law that keeps the children of God connected to their inheritance in the earth, and ensures they enjoy continuous prosperity and increase. He told the children of Israel never to appear before Him empty saying, *"...and none shall appear before me empty."* (Exo 23:15). *"...and they shall not appear before the Lord empty. Every man shall give as he is able according to the blessing of the Lord thy God which he has given thee."* (Deut 16:16-17). God wants His children to remain connected to the spiritual flow of his blessings.

He specifically tells his children, *"Honor the Lord with thy substance and with the first fruits of all thine increase: so, shall thy barns be filled with plenty and thy presses shall burst out with new wine."* (Proverbs 4:9-10), while the rest of the world is operating the 'seedtime and harvest' principle in the earth, the children of God are privileged to operate the same principle at a higher spiritual level with the author and source of everything himself (God). This is what safeguards the prosperity of God's children in a perverse world system. Unexplainable wealth has been characterized with the children of God through the years, and it will continue as long as we honor the Lord with our substance according to his word.

The Lord then specially commanded the children of Isreal to give a tithe of all the increase of their seed that the field brings forth every year saying, *"Thou shall truly tithe all the increase of thy seed that the field brings forth year by year."* (Deut 14:22). This He instructed saying, *"And all the tithe of the land whether of the seed of the land, or of the fruit of the tree, is the Lord's: it is holy unto the Lord."* (Lev 27:30). This meant that the tithe of all their increase belonged to God, it is holy, and they were to give it to him without excuse. That's why He told them where to take it saying, *"But the tithe of the children of Israel, which they offer as an heave offering unto the Lord, I have given to the Levites to inherit: therefore, I have said unto them, among the children of Israel they shall have no inheritance..."* (Num 18: 24-32), when they didn't give it He said they were robbing him, *"Will a man rob God? Yet you have robbed me. But you say wherein have we robbed thee? In tithes and offerings."* (Mal 3:8).

Notice that the tithe belongs to the Lord, and He gave it to the Levities (the Priests) for an inheritance. These where the ministers appointed by the Lord to do ministry unto the Lord on behalf of the children of Israel. They were to receive the tithe from the Israelites, and they too (the levities) were to take a tenth of the tithes received and give it to Aaron their priest. (Num 18:28).

The tithe was first revealed to Papa Abraham who was the first to give a tithe to one who is described as a priest of God. This priest by the name Melchizedek has no father or mother in brief his whereas about are unknown to anyone. He appeared to receive a tithe from Abraham, and we never hear from him again until the coming of Jesus whose priesthood is after the order of Melchizedek.

Hebrews 7:1-28 says, *"For this Melchizedek, King of Salem, priest of the most high God, who met Abraham returning from the slaughter of the kings and blessed him: To whom also Abraham gave a tenth part of all: first being by interpretation King of righteousness, and after that also King of Salem, which is King of Peace. Without father, without mother, without descent, having neither beginning of days, nor end of life; but made like unto the son of God; abideth a priest continually. Now, consider how great this man was, unto whom even the patriarch Abraham gave the tenth of the spoils... And without contradictions the less is blessed of the better... If therefore perfection were by the Levitical priesthood, (for under it the people received the law) what further need was there that another priest should rise after the order of Melchizedek, and not be called after the order of Aaron? For he of whom these things are spoken pertains to another tribe, of which no man gave attendance at the altar. For it is evident that our Lord sprang out of Juda; of which tribe Moses spoke nothing concerning priesthood. And it is yet far more evident; for that after the similitude of Melchizedek there arise another priest. Who is made not after the law of a carnal commandment, but after the power of an endless life. For he testifies, thou art a priest for ever after the order of Melchizedek. By so much was Jesus made a surety of a better testament... this man, because he continues forever, has an unchangeable priesthood."*

When you read the entire chapter 7 of Hebrews, you will fully understand that the priesthood did not start with the children of Israel under the law and neither did it end with them. We see a Priest Melchizedek appearing to Abraham and Abraham giving him a tithe of his spoils and Melchizedek the Priest blesses Abraham. Therefore, the idea of priesthood and the tithe was not a concept that came with the Law of Moses. The priesthood and the tithe were before the law. That's why the priesthood continues with Jesus in the New Testament as the High Priest not after the order of Aaron but after the order of Melchizedek the Priest of the most high God (Heb 5:4-6) to whom Abraham gave a tithe before his seed under the law were ever born.

* * *

A few things to note about the tithe.

1. The tithe belongs to God, and it is given to the Priest.

2. The tithe did not start with the law, Abraham who is the father of faith, the father of us all, introduced the tithe when he gave his tithe to the priest of God Melchiedek.

3. Thereafter, Abraham's generations were commanded by God to give tithe to the Priests among them. That Priesthood is later dissolved by the coming of another Priest — Jesus Christ, whose priesthood is after the order of the first Priest (Melchizedek) to receive tithe from Abraham our father.

4. The Bible says the priesthood of the last Priest, Jesus, is forever (Hebrews 6:20) just as Melchizedek's priesthood was and this last Priest Jesus, is our high priest today. (Hebrews 4:14-15).

5. We know that, Priests are ordained to offer sacrifices and Jesus our high priest offered himself for us once and for all. They also do intercede for the people which intercession Jesus our high priest does to this day through his blood that speaks a better covenant. And also, priests receive tithe from the people.

6. If our high priest Jesus offered the greatest sacrifice of all time, intercedes for us, and is after the order of Melchizedek the priest of God, of whom the only thing we know about is receiving tithe from Abraham; doesn't this mean that Jesus our high priest should also receive tithes from us in the same way that Melchizedek whom he takes after received tithe from our father Abraham.

7. And now that the church of Jesus Christ is referred to as a royal priesthood, made kings and priests unto God (Rev 1:5-6) and himself Jesus our High Priest; shouldn't we learn from the Levitical Priesthood

that was commanded to receive tithe and also give tithe to their High Priest Aaron? Shouldn't we as a body of priests give tithe to our High Priest Jesus? Weren't all these things written for our learning. (Rom 15:4).

8. God commanded the tithe to be given to the Priests in the places designated to be holy places of worship. Today the Priests that minister to God's people (Eph 4; 11-12) in the church of Jesus Christ the High Priest receive the tithe on His behalf.

9. The Priesthood and the tithe have evidently continued to us in the New Testament through Jesus Christ our Lord, who was declared by God a Priest forever after the order of Melchizedek. (Heb 5:5-6). Anyone giving tithe today is giving tithe to our High Priest Jesus Christ the head of the church, and whose priesthood remains forever.

10. The tithe is so important for the preservation and continuous flow of abundant blessings in our lives as children of God. God expects every one of his children to honor this spiritual instruction and give Him His tithe of every increase so that there will be food in His house. This is our primary financial involvement with the kingdom business in the earth, which enables the work of the kingdom to spread to the ends of the earth while keeping us plunged into divine blessings according to Malachi 3:10-12.

Our heavenly Father is a God who delights in the prosperity of his children. (Psalms 35:27). All our fathers the patriarchs were wealthy men of God. In fact, God promised the whole world to one man Abraham and that promise was fulfilled to all of us in Christ. *"For the promise, that he should be the heir of the world, was not to Abraham, or to his seed, through the law, but through the righteousness of faith...therefore it is of faith, that it might be by grace; to the end the promise might be sure to all the seed; not to that only which is of the law, but to that also which is of the faith of Abraham; who is the father of us all."* (Romans 4:13, 16)

And (Galatians 3:27-29) says, *"For as many of you as have been baptized into Christ have put on Christ. There is neither Jew nor Greek, there is neither bond nor free, there is neither male nor female; for ye are all one in Christ Jesus. And if ye be Christ's, then are ye Abraham's seed, and heirs according to the promise."*

The Earth and the fullness thereof belong to God and He has given it to us (Romans 8:16-17). Don't let anything or anyone cheat you out of your inheritance. Have a blessed mindset while consistently exercising the divine principles of increase stipulated for us in the scriptures, and you will stay above the unstable economic system of this world. In a nutshell, living by the word, closely walking with the Holy Spirit will keep you empowered to operate above the corruption in the world and keep you in constant supply of all things.

He says, *"But this I say: He who sows sparingly will also reap sparingly, and he who sows bountifully will also reap bountifully. Everyman according as he purposes in his heart, so let him give not grudgingly, or of necessity: for God loves a cheerful giver. And God is able to make all grace abound toward you; that you, always having all sufficiency in all things may abound to every good work. As it is written, he has dispersed abroad; he has given to the poor; his righteousness remains forever..."* (2 Cor 9:6-11).

Many of God's children have operated these principles and got themselves living in abundance going forward and upward only. Those that have ignored these principles will tell you; they have had to spend more than necessary on many occasions, in hospitals, accidents, theft, I mean the devourer showed up in all forms to devour their wealth and hinder progress because there was no protection or seed for increase. It doesn't matter how anyone may want to see it, but for the child of God, the journey should always be upward only, increase and multiplication only. No losses should be registered. *"The path of the just is as the shining light, that shines more and more unto the perfect day."* (Prov 4:18).

* * *

Conclusion

The word of God was given to us as an instruction manual for the life of God in us. The Bible clearly tells us that, *"Every scripture is God-breathed (given by His inspiration) and profitable for instruction, for reproof and conviction of sin, for correction of error and discipline in obedience, (and) for training in righteousness (in holy living in conformity to God's will in thought, purpose and action), so that the man of God may be complete and proficient, well fitted and thoroughly equipped for every good work."* (1 Tim 3:16-17)

God's word is God himself and everyone that desires to see God and live for Him, finds him in his word; and the transformation thereafter is for a lifetime. *"In the beginning was the word, and the word was with God and the word was God. The same was in the beginning with God. All things were made by him and without him was not anything made that was made. In him was life and the life was the light of men... that was the true light, which lighteth every man that cometh into this this world."* (John 1:1-9).

God's word created everything and is the only true light that lights everyone that comes into this world. Everything that we desire in life has its source in the word of God. The increase of grace, knowledge, power, peace, joy, just mention it, it's all in the word of God. When we make up our minds to choose the word of God over everything else, we will always be the story tellers of its power and glory!

He says in (Isaiah 66:1-2 NIV), *"Heaven is my throne, and the earth is my footstool; where is the house you will build for me? Where will my resting place be? Has not my hand made all these things and so they came into being? Declares the Lord; "this is the one I esteem; he who is humble and contrite in spirit and trembles at my word"* God almighty is letting us know that of all things he has made, the one person he honors, admires the most and esteems highly is that person who is humble in spirit and hears His word to do it.

King Solomon, after expounding on all the wisdom he knew, made a remarkable conclusion in (Ecclesiastes 12:13 AMP) saying, *"All has been heard; the end of the matter is; fear God (revere and worship Him, knowing He is) and keep His commandments, for this is the whole of man (the full original purpose of his creation, the object of God's providence, the root of character, the foundation of all happiness, the adjustment to all inharmonious circumstances and conditions under the sun) and the whole duty for every man."*

There it is, King Solomon said it in his conclusion of the matter! To fear God and keep his word is the whole duty of man. It is the original purpose of man's creation, where he will find all happiness, acquire character and enjoy God's provisions, care and sustenance. It sure can't get better than this!

* * *

Prayer of Salvation

In case you have been reading this book, and you are not yet born again, or you had walked away from the faith, now is the time to put things right with God. We believe this is your appointed time to receive this precious gift of eternal life and start a personal relationship with God almighty by wholeheartedly repeating the confession below:

Dear Father,

Thank you for loving me so much that you sent your only begotten son; that if I believe in him, I should never perish but have everlasting life.

Father as your word says that if we shall confess with our mouth the Lord Jesus and shall believe in our hearts that you have raised him from the dead, we shall be saved. According to Romans 10:9; right now I confess with my mouth that Jesus is my Lord and Savior, because I believe in my heart that he died for me and you raised him from the dead for my salvation. I now receive the forgiveness of all my sins in Jesus Name.

Thank you dear father for saving my life and for the precious gift of eternal life I have received now through Jesus Christ. I declare that I am born again. I am your child with your nature and life in me.

I belong to your kingdom now. I am a new creature, the old is gone, the new has come and all the new in me now is from you my God, in Jesus mighty name.

Amen.

Congratulations! You are now a child of God. You can reach us for more information through the contact address in this book. God richly bless you!

* * *